CW00665503

The Perfect Cup of Tea ISBN 978-0-9930773-1-9
Fisherton Press Ltd

www.fishertonpress.co.uk

First published in 2015 in the United Kingdom

Text and illustrations © Sonia Malik 2015

ISBN 978-0-9930773-1-9

A CIP catalogue record for this book is available from the British Library

The perfect cup of tea

Sonia Malik

My mummy drinks lots and lots of tea.

She drinks tea in the morning.

She drinks tea in the afternoon.

She even drinks tea in the evening!

My mummy says that people drink tea all over the world.

Families drink tea.

Prime ministers and presidents
drink tea.

Royal families drink tea.

They probably even drink tea in space!

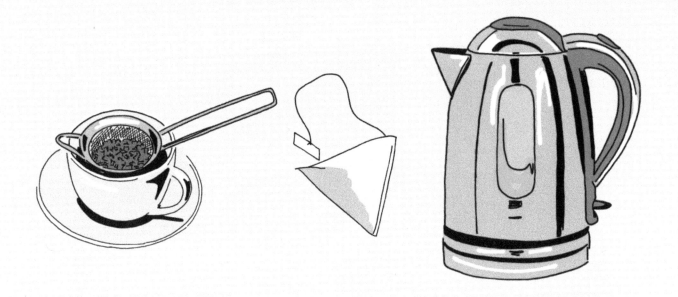

People make tea in lots of different ways.

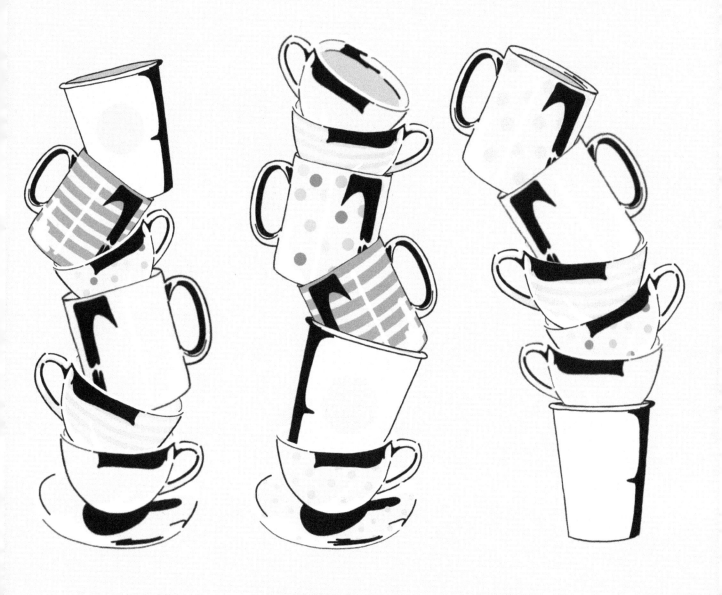

And drink it from lots
of different cups.

My mummy says that she makes the
perfect cup of tea.

She says making tea is like science.

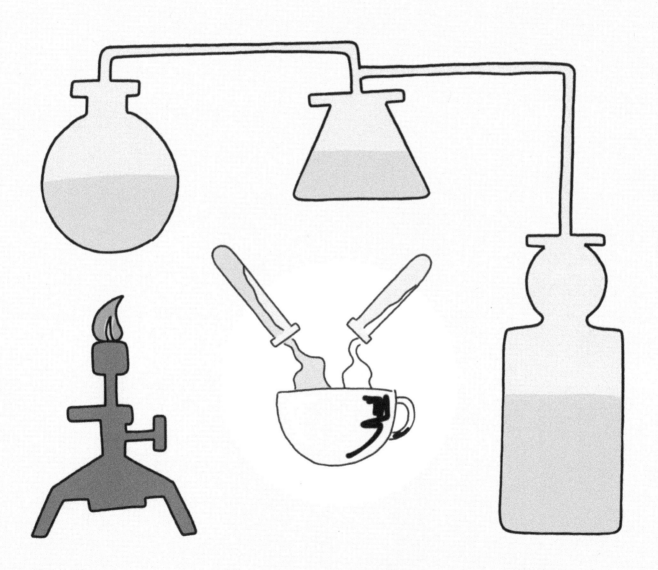

This is how she does it:

She always uses a teapot.

She uses hot hot water.

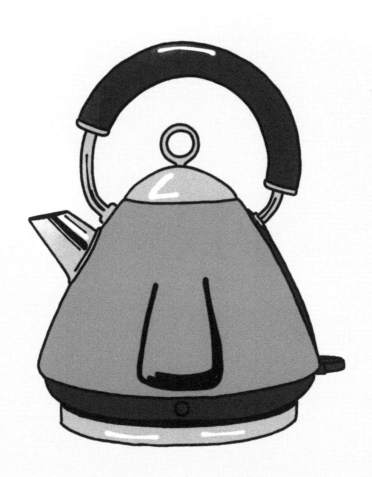

She makes it very strong.

And she keeps it warm with a tea cosy.

My mummy always puts the tea in before the milk.

But my daddy does it the other way round.

Some people don't use milk at all.

Some people make their tea sweet.

But in my house we just

drink it with a biscuit.

And that is how you make

the perfect cup of tea!

With thanks to George Orwell's 'A Nice Cup of Tea' for the inspiration behind the book.

If you enjoyed this book...

Tell:
- your local librarian
- your teacher
- your friends
- your local bookshop

Write:
- to us general@fishertonpress.co.uk
- blog about it
- on social media #FishertonPress
- review it online

Buy:
- a copy for a friend
- birthday presents
- other Fisherton books
- donate a book via our website

www.fishertonpress.co.uk

9 780993 077319